CLAUDIA MILLS

7 x 9 =
Trouble!

Pictures by
G. BRIAN KARAS

SQUARE
FISH

Farrar Straus Giroux
New York

SQUARE FISH

An Imprint of Macmillan
175 Fifth Avenue
New York, NY 10010
mackids.com

Library of Congress Cataloging-in-Publication Data
Mills, Claudia.
7 x 9 = trouble! / Claudia Mills ; pictures by G. Brian Karas.
p.   cm.
Summary: Third-grader Wilson struggles with his times-tables in order to beat the class deadline.
ISBN 978-0-374-46452-3
[1. Multiplication—Tables—Fiction. 2. Schools—Fiction. 3. Brothers—Fiction.]
I. Title: Seven times nine equals trouble! II. Karas, G. Brian, ill. III. Title.
PZ7.M69362 Aae 2002   [Fic]—dc21   2001016028

Originally published in the United States by Farrar Straus Giroux
First Square Fish Edition: February 2013
Square Fish logo designed by Filomena Tuosto

20 19

AR: 4.3 / LEXILE: 590L

To Marti Manning

7 x 9 = Trouble!

Wilson Williams searched through his desk for a pencil that didn't have a broken point and a chewed-off eraser. He found one that was pretty sharp, but the eraser had been bitten down to nothing. It would have to do.

Wilson knew he shouldn't chew his erasers. He did it only when he was nervous. Or bored. During math, doing multiplication, he was nervous *and* bored.

"All right, class," Mrs. Porter said. "You'll have two minutes for your times-table test." Wilson followed her eyes up to the creeping second hand on the classroom clock. "Ready, set, go!"

Wilson was doing the 3s. Some kids were already up to the 6s and the 7s. Wilson's best friend, Josh Hernandez, was up to the 5s. Laura Vicks was up to the 9s.

The 3s were hard enough for Wilson. He stared down at his paper. $3 \times 1 = 3$. That one wasn't bad. $3 \times 3 = 9$. But what was 3×8? Wilson couldn't remember. He wrote down 26, but that didn't look right. He tried to erase it with what was left of his eraser. It didn't erase.

Beside his desk, Squiggles, the class hamster, dozed in a pile of wood shavings. Squiggles was the best thing about third grade, Wilson thought. Squiggles, and art, and hanging out with Josh were all good things. Math was the worst thing. And multiplication was the worst thing about math. And daily times-table tests were the worst thing about multiplication.

Wilson gave up on 3×8. $3 \times 10 = 30$. $3 \times 11 = 33$. He came to another hard one: 3×7.

At least it was Friday, and Wilson was finally the person who was taking Squiggles home with him for the weekend. He and his little brother, Kipper, could hardly wait.

They had already planned it out. Wilson would give Squiggles his food; Kipper would give Squiggles his water. Squiggles would sleep in Wilson's room on Friday night and in Kipper's room on Saturday night. On Sunday night he'd sleep in Wilson's room again, but Kipper would get to hold him extra that evening.

Wilson wrote down 21 for the answer to 3×7. Or was it 22? He left it as it was. He skipped 3×9. $3 \times 0 = 0$. $3 \times 2 = 6$.

"Time!" Mrs. Porter called out. Wilson hadn't finished enough of the problems. He hadn't passed the 3s. Again.

From across the room, Josh was grinning. He must have finished all his 5s.

"Mrs. Porter, I think I passed my 9s!" Laura called out. "Can I stay after school and do my 10s and 11s? Then all I'll have is my 12s before I can get my ice cream cone."

Mrs. Porter let people stay after school to take extra times-table tests if they wanted to. Wilson couldn't imagine ever wanting to do that.

Mrs. Porter had promised an ice cream cone to everybody who passed all twelve times-table tests by March 16. Wilson had a feeling he wouldn't even be up to the 4s by March 16. It was almost the end of February; March 16 was just three weeks away.

He looked back at Squiggles. Squiggles was awake now, watching him, his eyes bright and beady, his curious little nose twitching. Wilson and Kipper didn't have a pet. Their mother didn't like pets. Wilson had to plead and beg for six months before she agreed to let Squiggles come home for the weekend.

As Wilson clucked softly to Squiggles, Mrs. Porter laid a piece of paper on his desk.

"Wilson, you still haven't passed your 3s." Her voice was low, but Wilson was sure half the class could hear. "I want you

to take this note to your parents so they can help you study at home."

Wilson stared down at it:

> Dear Parents,
>   We have been working hard on learning our multiplication. All third graders need to know the times tables up to 12 by Friday, March 16.
>   Your child _Wilson W._ has now passed his or her times tables through _2_.
>   Please help with lots of at-home practice.
>
> > Sincerely,
> > Carol Porter

There went the rest of Wilson's life. He hoped his parents wouldn't make him start his at-home practice this weekend. This weekend he'd be too busy playing with Squiggles.

As soon as the bell rang, Wilson ran outside to the kindergarten door to get Kipper. For once, Kipper was ready, although he was missing one mitten.

"Where's your mitten?"

"I don't know." Kip's mouth pulled down as if he might cry. Kipper cried a lot.

"Is it in your pocket? That's where it was the last hundred times you couldn't find it."

Kipper checked. His face lit up. "One hundred and one," he said happily. Unlike Wilson, Kipper was good at math, at least at easy little kindergarten math. He could already count past one hundred.

"Do you have Snappy and Peck-Peck?" They were Kipper's favorite beanbag animals. Wilson knew from experience that it was a terrible thing if they were ever left behind.

For answer, Kipper unzipped his jacket partway. A little alligator head and a little penguin head poked out.

"Okay," Wilson said. "Let's go get Squiggles!"

The boys raced back to Wilson's classroom.

Mrs. Porter handed the bags of food and litter to Kipper and helped Wilson pick up Squiggles's cage. "Are you sure you can carry all this?" she asked. "How far do you have to walk?"

"Just three blocks."

Wilson's mother had offered to come and get them. She worked part-time in a dentist's office, so she was home most days after school. But Wilson had wanted the glory of carrying Squiggles home. He wanted everyone in the neighborhood to see him strolling down the street with Squiggles, as if Squiggles were *his* hamster, who only came to third grade once in a while for some new adventures.

"All right," Mrs. Porter said. "Have a great time, Squiggles! I'm sure Wilson and Kipper will take very good care of you."

Slowly, Wilson carried Squiggles down the hall and out the doors of Hill Elementary. Kipper's face shone with the honor of being his assistant.

It would have been the proudest moment of Wilson's third-grade year except for Mrs. Porter's note in his backpack. One note plus ten more times tables would equal three weeks of nothing but trouble.

Wilson's mother handed him another times-table test. His father got ready to click his stopwatch. Kipper and Squiggles and Snappy and Peck-Peck sat watching him.

"All right," his father said. "Three, two, one, start!"

Wilson began racing through the practice test. At least at home his pencil had a freshly sharpened point and a whole pink eraser. If he could get a perfect score this time, he could go back to playing with Squiggles. He and Kipper had built a maze out of wooden blocks for Squiggles. So far Squiggles wasn't much better at the maze than Wilson was at the times-table tests.

He forced himself to focus on the practice test, but when his dad called out "Time!" he still hadn't finished.

His mother peered at his test. Then she exchanged a look with his father. Wilson tried to exchange a look with Squiggles, but now he was asleep on the towel on Kipper's lap, apparently worn out from his morning in the maze.

"Let's try this another way," his dad said. "Multiplying by 3 is just like counting by 3s. Let's hear you count by 3s."

"3, 6, 9, 12 . . . um, 12 . . . um . . . 15 . . . um . . ."

"Peck-Peck can count by 3s," Kipper said.

"Honey, we need to be quiet so Wilson can concentrate," their mother said.

As if anyone could concentrate on math with an audience of two parents, one little brother, one hamster, one beanbag alligator, and one beanbag penguin. Only Squiggles was any real help to Wilson, and Wilson wasn't even getting to hold him.

"Don't you want Peck-Peck to count?" Kipper asked. "When Peck-Peck counts, he counts fish, because penguins eat fish."

"Let's hear him," Wilson said. He was tired of concentrating.

"3 fish, 6 fish, 9 fish, 12 fish, 15 fish, 18 fish, 21 fish, 24 fish, 27 fish, 30 fish—"

"That's enough, Kipster," their dad said.

"No, wait," their mom said. "Did you

hear him, Jon? He just counted all the way to 30 by 3s." Wilson could tell his mother was impressed. He was impressed, too, though he wasn't about to show it.

"Snappy can count by 4s," Kipper said. "But he doesn't count fish because he doesn't eat fish."

"What does Snappy eat?" Wilson asked, hoping Kipper would start telling some long story about Snappy's favorite foods and forget about counting.

Kipper gave a mischievous grin. "He eats penguins." He made Peck-Peck's head turn around in indignation.

One of Kipper's games was to make Snappy and Peck-Peck squabble like two cartoon characters, the kind who were always cheerfully trying to blow each other up with dynamite. Wilson thought it was a strange game, but Kipper seemed to like it. And Snappy and Peck-Peck always ended up as friends.

Kipper went on: "That's what Snappy eats, Peck-Peck. It's his favorite food. Penguins. Four at a time. 4 penguins, 8 penguins, 12 penguins, 16 penguins, 20 penguins, 24 penguins . . . What comes after 24? Oh, 28 penguins."

Kipper made Peck-Peck lunge at Snappy. "Peck! Peck!" Peck-Peck attacked Snappy with his little plastic beak. "That's what penguins do to alligators, peck them!"

"Kipper, how am I supposed to do my multiplication when you're making so much noise?" Wilson asked crossly. Not that he wanted to do multiplication.

"What's multiplication? Is it something for penguins?"

Kipper was trying to act cute. Wilson

thought he was just being annoying. He wondered what Kipper would have done if he had been born first and not gotten to be the baby.

"I'll show you," their dad said. He took a handful of buttons from the jar they kept in the kitchen to help Wilson with math homework. As he showed Kipper how to multiply 2 × 3 and 3 × 4, Wilson drew pictures of Squiggles in the margins of his paper.

"I get it," Kipper said. "So 2 penguins times 3 penguins is 6 penguins. Six yummy penguins. Peck-Peck, Snappy is going to eat six penguins! I like multiplying! Do you like multiplying, Wilson?"

"No," Wilson said. He hadn't liked multiplication an hour ago, and he didn't like it any more now that his baby brother could do it better than he could.

"All right, Kipper, we need to get back to work now," their father said. "Try to count by 3s again, Will."

"I can't do it when everybody's listening," Wilson said. He glared at Kipper. For good measure, he glared at Peck-Peck and Snappy, too. He hoped Squiggles didn't think he was glaring at him.

"Kipper, why don't you take Peck-Peck and Snappy and go play somewhere else?" their mother asked.

"I want to be with Wilson," Kipper said. "Peck-Peck and Snappy want to help him do his math."

"Come on, Kipper," their mother coaxed. "We need to get this done."

"Yeah, Kipper, you keep making me mess up," Wilson said. He knew it wasn't true, but he felt better saying it anyway.

"I do not!" Kipper's lower lip quivered. "I wasn't bothering, just watching."

"*And* counting fish and penguins and other dumb things."

"How about a story?" their mother asked then. "I'll read to you while Daddy helps Wilson with his math. Kipper, let's go pick out a story."

"Leave Squiggles here," Wilson said. He grabbed Squiggles, towel and all, out of Kipper's lap. He tried to settle him on his own lap, but Squiggles squirmed so badly that Wilson had to put him in his cage. So Kipper had spoiled his fun with Squiggles, too.

In tears now, clutching Peck-Peck and Snappy, one in each hand, Kipper left the kitchen with their mom.

Wilson was glad Kipper was leaving,

but not that he was crying. No one could look more little and pathetic when he cried than Kipper. Still, counting by fish! Counting by penguins! There could be nothing dumber than that, Wilson thought.

Except being three years older and not being able to count by 3s at all.

On Monday morning, Wilson gave Squiggles an extra lettuce leaf and carrot stick for his breakfast. He hated the thought of taking Squiggles back to school. The pictures he had drawn of Squiggles covered half of the refrigerator. But if Squiggles didn't go back to school, Wilson would miss him there, too. He had a feeling he could pass the 3s test today if Squiggles were squeaking and cuddling beside him.

"Boys, it's time to go!" their mother called out.

Kipper zipped Snappy and Peck-Peck into his pockets and grabbed the bags of food and litter. Wilson picked up Squiggles's cage.

Carrying Squiggles back to school was less fun than carrying him home, but it was still fun. As Wilson walked, he chanted the 3s to himself. If only Mrs. Porter would do the times-table tests first thing in the morning, before he could forget anything!

When they reached school, Kipper ran off to see his kindergarten friends. Wilson met Josh on the playground.

"Bad morning," Josh said, instead of "Good morning."

Wilson laughed. Josh was always Mr. Negativity.

"What's bad about it?"

"One: My mother says if I don't pass the 6s today, I can't watch TV all week. Two: I don't know my 6s. Three: Well, two is enough, don't you think?"

"I haven't passed my 3s yet," Wilson admitted.

"Are your parents ready to kill you?"

"No." That was one good thing about Wilson's parents. They had made him do a zillion practice tests that weekend, but they hadn't yelled.

"You're lucky. I'd be dead already. 'Here lies Josh. He's dead, by gosh.' "

"Do one for me," Wilson said. Josh was good at funny rhymes.

" 'Here lies Wilson Williams.' " Josh thought for a minute. "Williams. Williams. 'At his funeral there were millions.' "

Laura Vicks walked by with Becca

Landry. If Laura passed her 12s today, she would be the first one in the class to get her ice cream cone.

Josh kept on rhyming under his breath: " 'Here lies Laura Vicks. She thinks she's so smart, but she makes me sick.' 'Here lies Becca Landry.' Landry . . . Bandry . . . Candry. 'She exploded from too much candy.' "

The bell rang. Wilson picked up Squiggles's cage. Josh took the bags that Kipper had left beside it.

" 'Here lies Squiggles . . .' "

"Don't make one for Squiggles." Wilson couldn't bear to think of anything happening to Squiggles, even in a silly rhyme.

"How about: 'Long live Squiggles. He is cute although he wiggles.' "

Wilson liked that one.

Mrs. Porter helped Wilson get Squiggles settled in his corner. "You look as if you had a great weekend, Squiggles!" she said.

"I'm going to pass my 3s today," Wilson told her with more confidence than he felt. $3 \times 7 = 21$. $3 \times 8 = 24$. $3 \times 9 = 27$. All he had to do was remember them until math time at two o'clock.

That afternoon, in social studies, they were making relief maps of Colorado. Wilson loved making maps, and relief maps were the best kind. He felt lucky to live in a state with lots of mountains. It would be boring to make a relief map of a state that was perfectly flat.

Six at a time, the students took turns at the craft table. Wilson was glad that Josh was in his group. Laura was in his group, too. Wilson knew even Laura's map would not be as good as his. Too bad Mrs. Porter didn't give an ice cream cone to the person who made the best map in the class.

Carefully, Wilson molded his Rocky Mountains from the floury paste mixed by the parent helper.

"Nice job, Wilson," Mrs. Porter said as she walked by.

The paste felt good between Wilson's fingers. He could see why Squiggles spent so much time making little nests in his wood shavings. It was satisfying to make something with your hands, or your paws.

When Wilson was finished with his map, his Rockies looked truly majestic. Josh's were a little too far to the east. Laura's were lumpy, like the gobs of tooth-paste that hardened in the sink at home after Kipper had brushed his teeth. Maybe if you knew 12×9, it didn't matter if your Rocky Mountains looked like toothpaste gobs.

Proudly, Wilson carried his map over to the floor by Squiggles's cage to dry. They would paint them tomorrow. On his way to wash his hands, Wilson reviewed the hardest 3s again: $3 \times 7 = 21$, $3 \times 8 = 24$, $3 \times 9 = 27$. Bingo!

There was still five minutes before recess, time to hold Squiggles just once before he and Josh went outside to play. Holding Squiggles would give him good luck on the test.

Squiggles wasn't in his cage! The door was open. Was someone else holding him? It better not be Laura. She didn't need good luck on her test. Disappointed, Wilson looked around the room, but saw no soft furry ball on anybody's lap.

Then, glancing down at the floor, Wilson saw him. Squiggles had gotten out of his cage. He was on the floor, smack in the middle of the drying relief maps of Colorado. And, sure enough, out of all the relief maps, he was sitting right on top of Wilson's. Wilson had always known Squiggles was smart.

"Squiggles!" Wilson scolded good-naturedly.

Squiggles let Wilson pick him up. His fur was a bit gooey from the flour paste. When Squiggles was back in his cage, Wilson did a quick repair job on his mountains. Once again, they towered above the plains.

After recess, Wilson passed his 3s. Josh didn't pass his 6s. It would be a long week without TV at Josh's house.

" 'Here lies Josh's TV,' " Josh said

glumly as they waited together after school for Kipper. " 'It's turned off. Poor, poor me.' "

Wilson couldn't share Josh's gloom. Three times tables down. Only—Wilson counted on his fingers—nine more to go.

Wilson passed the 4s on Wednesday, and the 5s on Friday. The 5s were pretty easy; he already knew most of them from telling time. During the weekend, his parents coached him on the 6s, and he managed to pass those on Monday.

Then came the 7s.

Wilson could not learn his 7s.

"Each times table is easier than the one before," his father said encouragingly.

Wrong. Each times table was *harder* than the one before. Bigger numbers were harder than little numbers. The pile of 7s tests Wilson had failed was proof of that.

"Take the 7s," his father said. Wilson wished somebody *would* take the 7s, take them far away and bury them in a deep dark hole. "Because you've already passed the first six tables, you have a head start on the 7s. You already know 7×1, 7×2, 7×3, 7×4, 7×5, and 7×6."

It sounded good, but somehow it didn't work when Wilson sat down to take the test. Just because he knew 4×7 didn't mean he knew 7×4. Everything felt different when the numbers were turned around.

Besides, Wilson didn't *completely* remember the times tables he had passed. It was easy to forget number facts when you weren't practicing them every single day, ten times in a row.

Anyway, the hardest 7s were 7×8 and 7×9, not to mention 7×12. It was too much to expect people to know things times 12.

Suddenly Wilson had an idea. "I bet I could learn them if I had a pet," he told his mother. He *had* learned his times tables better when Squiggles was home with him.

"We've already talked about this," his mother said. "Pets are work. Pets are responsibility."

"I can do work. I can take responsibility. I took good care of Squiggles when he came home, didn't I?"

His mother didn't answer.

Josh was struggling with his times tables, too. "I told you the 7s were hard," he grumbled as they hung upside down on the climbing structure at morning recess on Thursday. Josh was now stuck on his 9s.

"Five kids in our class have gotten their ice cream cones," Wilson said. Laura had been first, of course.

"I don't think the cones look all that great," Josh said. "They're the cheapo kind that come in a carton, with sticky paper smushed over the top of each one. They're not the real kind you get at the ice cream store."

Wilson didn't care which kind of cones they were. He wasn't likely to get one anytime soon.

That night at home, Wilson got ready to take some more practice tests, ignoring Kipper as best he could. At least Kipper had stopped counting fish and penguins,

though Wilson had seen him working away on his own little practice charts of 2s and 3s.

"Can I do the stopwatch?" Kipper begged.

"Okay," their dad said before Wilson could object. "Thanks for wanting to help, Kipper."

Wilson sighed heavily, but no one seemed to notice.

Their dad showed Kipper how to use the stopwatch and then left the boys alone to practice while he went into the kitchen and poured himself a root beer. Wilson could hear it fizzing against the ice cubes in the glass. His mouth felt dry.

"All right," Kipper said importantly. "Ready, set, go!"

Wilson started tearing through the sheet of 7s.

"Wait," Kipper said. "I pushed the wrong button."

Wilson put down his pencil, trying not to show his impatience. This would have been his best score yet, he knew it. He tore the spoiled test in half, a little more forcefully than he needed to. He felt like shredding it into litter for Squiggles's cage.

"Okay," Kipper said. "I know how to do it now."

Wilson picked up another blank test. His father had printed a huge stack of them on the computer. He must have expected Wilson to fail a lot of 7s tests, judging from the thickness of the stack. Wilson gripped his pencil.

"Ready, set, go!"

Wilson launched himself into the test again. He scribbled down answers as fast as he could write. He could tell he was doing great. He was getting more problems done in two minutes than he had ever done before. For the first time ever, since he had started doing times-table tests, he got the whole entire sheet completed before anyone called time.

Suddenly Wilson felt suspicious. "Isn't it two minutes yet?"

Kipper looked down at the stopwatch. "It says three minutes, eleven seconds."

"Kipper! You're supposed to call time when it's exactly two minutes."

Kipper's face screwed up. That was Kipper's system. First he did something wrong. Then, when Wilson tried to point this out to him, he started to cry.

"Can I do it again? Please? I promise I'll do everything perfect."

Wilson considered. "One more time."

Kipper's cheerfulness returned. He usually perked up as soon as he got his way. "Peck-Peck is going to help me push the buttons."

Wilson groaned.

"Ready?"

Wilson made himself pick up his hundredth blank test from the pile. He watched as Kipper held Peck-Peck's shabby black flipper on the stopwatch button. How many boys in America were at this moment taking a times-table test administered by a beanbag penguin?

"Set?"

If Peck-Peck messed this one up, Wilson would kill him.

"Go!"

Wilson tried to concentrate on the test, he really did. But he didn't trust Kipper *or* Peck-Peck to time it right. He glanced up once to make sure Kipper was still checking the stopwatch. Peck-Peck's beady black eyes stared back at him.

What was 7×9? That was the one Wilson could never remember. And 7×6. It had to be the same as 6×7, which had been on the 6s test on Monday. But it seemed an eternity since Wilson had passed his 6s. It seemed an eternity since Wilson had passed anything.

"Time!" Kipper called out in the special gruff, growly voice he used for Peck-Peck. As if penguins growled. Someone should explain to Kipper the difference between a penguin and a bear.

Their dad reappeared, root beer in hand. He quickly scanned the test.

"Nope," he said regretfully. "But thanks for helping, Kipster. *And* Peck-Peck."

Yeah, Wilson thought. Thanks a lot.

5

Josh came to Wilson's house to play on Saturday.

Wilson wished he could go to Josh's house instead. Josh's house was more fun than Wilson's for several reasons:

1. Josh had a dog. Wilson didn't.
2. Josh had video games. Wilson didn't.

3. Josh didn't have a little brother. Wilson did.

But Wilson's mother said, "It isn't fair to Josh's family if you go there all the time and he never comes here. It's time for us to return the favor."

Wilson didn't like the way she said that. It sounded as if Josh's family was doing Wilson's family a favor by taking Wilson for a few hours every so often. Taking Wilson wasn't a favor. Taking *Kipper* would be a favor.

"So what should we do?" Wilson asked Josh as they plopped down in front of the turned-off TV. Wilson's mother said there was no point in having a friend over if you were just going to watch TV. That was another reason Wilson liked Josh's house better:

4. Josh could watch TV on play
dates. Wilson couldn't.

"We could play Candy Land," Kipper
suggested.

Wilson shot Kipper a furious look. How
come Kipper always hung around when
Wilson had a friend over? Wilson didn't
hang around with Kipper's friends.

"Or Chutes and Ladders?"

"No!"

Wilson's mother appeared. "Come with
me, Kipper. Wilson wants to be with his
friend for a while."

Wilson shot her a quick, grateful smile.

"Josh is my friend, too," Kipper insisted.
He looked pleadingly at Josh.

"You bet I am," Josh said.

Wilson's spirits sank. Josh was always
nice to little kids. It was a lot easier to be

nice to a little kid when the little kid wasn't your brother.

"And before I go I'll play a game with you, okay?" Josh went on. "But now Wilson and I have some boring big-kid stuff we have to do."

Wilson's spirits rose again as Kipper reluctantly followed their mother out of the room.

Then Wilson said, "So what *should* we do?"

"I don't know. What do you want to do?"

"I don't know. What do *you* want to do?"

"Nothing," Josh said.

That was all Wilson could think of, too. So they lay on their backs on the family-room floor, side by side, doing nothing.

Wilson's father came in. "Hard week, boys?" he asked with a chuckle.

Wilson didn't see any humor in his father's remark. It *had* been a hard week. A week in which you passed the 7s was a hard week, if any week was. And Josh had passed his 9s. They had earned the right to lie on the floor doing nothing.

"How about going outside and playing catch?" Wilson's father asked. "We have an extra glove you can use, Josh."

Catch was the last thing Wilson felt like doing. Well, it was the third-last thing, after Candy Land and Chutes and Ladders.

"Um—maybe later," Josh said politely.

"How are your times tables coming along?" Wilson's father asked Josh then, as if times tables were Josh's favorite topic of conversation. "Have you gotten that ice cream cone yet?"

"No," Josh said. "But I'm up to my 10s,

and they're easy. The 11s are easy, too. So all I really have left is my 12s."

"If you two get bored, you can always give each other times-table tests," Wilson's father said, finally turning to go upstairs. Wilson was pretty sure he was joking. "The stopwatch is over there on the table."

"You have a stopwatch?" Josh asked. "Cool! Let's go outside and time each other doing stuff."

They raced for the front door, ignoring Kipper, who watched them forlornly from the kitchen.

Wilson timed Josh racing to the corner and back. Twenty-five seconds.

Josh timed Wilson jumping on his pogo stick. Forty-six jumps in sixty seconds.

Wilson timed Josh retying his shoe,

which had come untied. Josh's shoes always came untied. Eighteen seconds.

So there was one good thing about Wilson's house, compared to Josh's:

    1. Wilson had a stopwatch. Josh
    didn't.

When they ran out of things to time,
they went inside for cookies and milk. The
cookies weren't Wilson's favorite kind. Wilson's mother bought cookies she didn't
like so she wouldn't eat them and gain
weight. The trouble was that the cookies
she didn't like, nobody else liked, either.
Wilson was back to reasons to go to Josh's
house:

    5. Josh had Oreos. Wilson
    didn't.

"Who made all the pictures of Squiggles?" Josh asked, looking at the refrigerator.

"I did," Wilson said. He wished he had Squiggles now, instead of just pictures of him.

"Wow," Josh said. "You really can draw."

Wilson felt himself flushing with pleasure at the praise.

"Can we play Candy Land yet?" Kipper begged, his mouth covered with cookie crumbs.

Josh looked at Wilson. "Soon," Wilson said. "Josh and I have a couple of other important things we have to do first."

"Like what?" Kipper asked suspiciously. "If you're going to do the stopwatch, you can time me. You can time me hopping."

Kipper started to hop in place in the kitchen, as if warming up for his record-breaking event.

Wilson tried to think of something they could time that Kipper couldn't do.

Unfortunately, Josh had an idea first. "Wilson and I need to practice our times tables. And then I'll play *two* games of Candy Land. I promise."

"I can do times tables," Kipper announced proudly. "I can do the 0s, and the 1s, and the 2s."

Josh looked taken aback. "Well, Wilson and I need to do the hard ones." He lowered his voice. "The *really* hard ones."

Shooting an apologetic look at Wilson, Josh led the flight to the family room.

"Why'd you have to say *that*?" Wilson grumbled to Josh. He could see Kipper spying on them from the kitchen.

"It just popped into my head," Josh said gloomily. "We'll time each other doing one test each, and then I guess it'll be Candy Land time."

Talk about something to look forward to.

Wilson picked up an 8s test from the pile for himself and a 12s test for Josh. Wilson's father had already printed out all the tests up to 12. Wilson could see himself in the middle of July, sitting by the side of the pool, still trying to finish his 12s.

"Ready?" Josh asked him.

Wilson picked up his pencil. "Uh-huh."

Even Candy Land was better than this. Wilson had thought of the final reason they should have gone to Josh's house:

6. Josh didn't have times-table
    tests. Wilson did.

Wilson passed his 8s on Monday. His dad remembered a little rhyme for the 8 he had found hardest when he was a boy: "An 8 and an 8 fell on the floor. Pick them up, and it's 64." 8 × 8 = 64. Bingo! And at least 8s were fun to decorate. Wilson could draw one funny face in the top half of an 8, and another funny face in the bottom half.

Josh passed his 12s the same day. Wilson saw Mrs. Porter give Josh a big smile as she laid the corrected quiz back on his desk.

"Good for you, Josh!" she said. "Do you want your ice cream cone after school or now, at recess?"

"Now," Josh said. He gave his lips a big smack, as if tasting the ice cream cone already. Wilson's pleasure in passing his 8s began to evaporate. He didn't know why Josh was acting so eager for the cone. He had already said they were just the crummy kind that came in a carton.

Mrs. Porter gave Wilson a smile, too, not as big as the smile she had given Josh. "You've been working hard, Wilson," she said. "You're almost there."

Wilson didn't think he was "almost there." The 9s lay before him like the towering Rockies on his relief map of Colorado. And he had to have all twelve times tables done by Friday.

As the class got up to go to recess, some of the boys high-fived Josh. Wilson knew he should, too. So he held his hand up the way the others did. Grinning, Josh smacked it hard.

Usually Wilson liked hard high-fives, but today the sting in his palm made him mad. "That hurt," he said.

"Sorry," Josh said, but he didn't sound crushed by guilt. He sounded like someone who was thrilled to be done with times-table tests forever.

"Do you want to go get my cone with me?" Josh asked. The cones were kept in the big metal freezer in the school kitchen. Wilson had watched from the hallway the day Laura Vicks had gotten hers.

"Nah," Wilson said, trying to sound

cheerful. How could Josh think Wilson would want to see him get his ice cream cone? Was Wilson supposed to watch him eat it, too?

"I'm going to stay here and play with Squiggles," Wilson said.

"Okay." Josh took off like a shot.

Wilson knew he should be happy for Josh, but he couldn't be. What if he couldn't pass all his times-table tests by Friday? He imagined himself finishing up in a couple of years, when he was a huge, hulking fifth grader, practically a grown man. His ice cream cone would still be sitting, forgotten, in a corner of the freezer.

He could almost see it, frozen in a solid block of ice formed from thousands of ice cube trays dripping on it over the years. Unless by then the custodian had thrown it away.

Wilson blinked back tears. "Here, Squiggles," he said as he fumbled at the latch on Squiggles's cage. Gently he scooped Squiggles up and held his furry body close. He should have been born a hamster, with nothing to do but ride around in a little Ferris wheel all day.

"I know a fun game to play with Squiggles." Laura Vicks had come up behind him. She hadn't gone out to recess, either. Laura often stayed inside to check her perfect work one more time, or to make her neat desk even neater.

"Sit down on the floor," Laura said. "Spread your legs out like this, in a big V."

Wilson did as she said.

Laura sat down facing him and made her own legs into another V. With her feet touching his feet, their legs made a narrow diamond.

"Now put Squiggles down inside. This is like a cage for Squiggles."

Wilson put Squiggles in the middle of the diamond. Right away Squiggles ran around trying to get out. He seemed to know it was a game. He stopped and looked right at Wilson, his small nose twitching. Then he tried to climb over Wilson's ankles. His sharp claws tickled through Wilson's sock.

Despite his misery, Wilson laughed. Laura laughed, too. As Squiggles managed to pull himself onto Wilson's leg, Wilson placed him carefully back in the diamond again.

"Are you up to the 9s?" Laura asked then.

Wilson nodded, his pleasure in the game slipping away. The whole school must know he hadn't passed his 9s yet.

Even Kipper's little kindergarten friends probably pointed at him when he walked by: "That's the boy who still hasn't passed his 9s."

"I know a trick for the 9s," Laura said. "Do you want me to show you?"

When Wilson didn't say no, Laura said, "It goes like this."

She held up ten fingers. "One times nine is nine." She put down her thumb. "See, you put down one finger, and nine fingers are left."

Wilson kept on watching.

"Two times nine is eighteen." Laura put her thumb back up again, and this time put her second finger down. "See, the thumb makes one, and then the other fingers make eight. Eighteen."

Wilson could sort of see it.

"Three times nine is twenty-seven."

This time Laura put down her third finger and showed Wilson that there was one group of two fingers and one group of seven fingers left: twenty-seven.

Laura used her fingers to go all the way to 9 × 9. Sure enough, she could show every 9s fact on her fingers. Wilson still added and subtracted on his fingers sometimes. He was glad to find out you could multiply on your fingers, too. He liked doing things with his hands.

Wilson had been so busy watching Laura's fingers, he hadn't been paying attention to Squiggles. In the nick of time, he caught Squiggles escaping over his knee.

"Squiggles, you rascal!" he said, laughing. Wilson liked the word. His grandfather was always calling Kipper a rascal.

The other kids were coming in from recess. Wilson put Squiggles back in his cage.

"Hey, Squiggs," Josh said as he passed Wilson and Squiggles on the way to his desk.

Wilson saw the faint trace of an ice cream mustache on Josh's upper lip. But he didn't mind. The 9s didn't seem like the Rocky Mountains anymore.

On Wednesday, Wilson passed *three* times-table tests: the 9s, the 10s, the 11s. He wondered if he had set a world record for the most times-table tests ever passed by one person in a single day.

"Nope," Josh said flatly when Wilson suggested this. They were standing together after school outside the kindergarten door, waiting for Kipper. "Laura passed *five* tests in one day, on the first day we started taking them. She did the 0s, the 1s, the 2s, the 3s, and the 4s, all in ten minutes."

It figured. Still, Wilson was grateful to Laura for showing him the 9s trick. He couldn't hate her for having snatched his world record away. Plus, passing three tests in one day was still pretty terrific, world record or no world record. Even Squiggles had looked extra happy when Wilson had taken him out of his cage to celebrate.

The kindergarten door opened, and Kipper came bursting out, first in line.

"Guess what?" he said.

Wilson didn't bother to guess. Usually when Kipper had news, it was that his teacher had read the class a story about penguins and he was going to tell Peck-Peck. Or that he had drawn a picture of an alligator in art and he was going to tell Snappy.

"I showed Mrs. Macky how I can multiply by 2s, and she said she's going to send me to a special math group with a bunch of first graders!"

Wilson's own big news didn't seem so big anymore. Wilson had never been picked to be in a special math group, and never would be. Even though he had done so well in math today, he still expected to be the last kid in their class to get his ice cream cone. *If* he ever got it. Everybody said the 12s were the worst. Wilson had heard Becca say the 12s were harder than all the others put together.

With Wilson's luck, Kipper would tear through the times tables in his special math group and get *his* cone before the end of kindergarten. Kipper would be merrily dripping his cone all over Snappy and Peck-Peck, while Wilson's cone was getting buried in ice in the school freezer.

"That's great, Kip," Josh said, since Wilson hadn't said anything. "See you guys tomorrow."

"When we get home, will you show me the 3s?" Kipper asked Wilson as they started walking.

"No," Wilson said. He tried to keep his voice patient and reasonable. "Because I have to work on my 12s. And I have ten spelling sentences to write. And I have to start on my shoebox diorama of a Colorado mammal."

If only there were a funny rhyme or magic trick for the 12s. But deep down, Wilson knew there wasn't. He was going to have to get over that last mountain range on his own. Somehow.

"Can Peck-Peck be in the shoebox diorama?" Kipper asked. "Are penguins Colorado mammals?"

"No!" Some questions simply could not be answered in a patient and reasonable way.

At home, Wilson's mother made a fuss over Kipper's news, as Wilson had known she would.

"How did you do on your 9s, honey?" she asked Wilson then.

"I passed them."

"Great! Do you want me to time you on your 10s?"

"I passed them, too. And the 11s."

"Wilson, that's wonderful!" She tried to draw him into a hug, but he pulled away.

"Not really."

"Of course it is. Three times tables in one day! I bet that's a record."

"Get real, Mom," Wilson snapped. Passing three times-table tests in one day might be a record for kindergarten. Not for third grade.

"Honey," his mom said gently, "your dad and I are both very proud of how hard you've worked. Some things come easily for some people. Look at how good you are at art. Some things take more time. And we're proud of you for putting in the time."

Wilson turned away. He felt as if he might cry.

Unfortunately, Wilson wasn't finished putting in time. And the more Wilson tried to study his 12s that afternoon, the more Kipper got in his way.

"Did you know that Ben T. wears size twelve underwear?"

"No!" Wilson hadn't known that and didn't need to know.

"Isaac L. wears size eight. I wear size six."

Did kindergartners really have nothing better to do with their time than compare underwear?

"Go away, Kipper. The 12s are hard. And I have to learn them by Friday." Sitting on the family-room couch, Wilson stared down at his paper.

"Do you want me to time you?"

"No, I want you to go away."

"What size underwear do you wear? Can I go check in your drawer?"

Wilson had had enough. "Mom! Kipper's bothering me!"

Kipper got a smug look on his face. "Mom!" he called out, his voice imitating Wilson's. "Wilson's tattling on me!"

Their mother came into the room. She didn't like tattling. "Kipper, stop bothering

Wilson," she said, sounding tired and frazzled. "Come along with me to the kitchen."

Before Kipper followed her, he arranged Snappy and Peck-Peck to keep Wilson company. Snappy was perched on Wilson's right knee; Peck-Peck was perched on Wilson's left knee.

As soon as Kipper was out of sight, Wilson gave his knees a mighty heave. But it made him feel bad to see Snappy and Peck-Peck lying facedown on the floor. So he picked them up and stuck them at the bottom of the couch.

Stuffed animals weren't company. *Real* animals were company. If only Squiggles could come home with Wilson every weekend, and every day after school, and on winter break, and spring break, and summer vacation. If only Wilson had a pet of his own, to keep him company all the year through.

Wilson walked into the kitchen to find his mother.

"I thought you needed peace and quiet to study without Kipper bothering you," his mother said.

"What I need is a pet," Wilson said. "I need a dog, or a cat, or a bunny, or a guinea pig, or a hamster."

"We'll see," his mother said.

Wilson and Kipper exchanged looks, their quarrel forgotten. It was the first time their mother hadn't said no. "We'll see" usually ended up meaning "No." But there was a small space between "We'll see" and "No" that was just big enough for hope to creep in.

When Wilson stumbled out of bed Thursday morning, he heard his parents talking in the kitchen. Their voices sounded low and discouraged.

". . . working so hard . . ." he thought he heard his mother say.

". . . maybe we should . . ." he thought he heard his father say.

They had to be talking about him, and his times tables. They probably thought it was hopeless to expect him to pass them by Friday. Just one more day! Maybe they thought they should send him to the resource room for tutoring. Or have him repeat a grade. Would he have to do third grade over again if he couldn't pass his 12s by June?

They stopped talking as soon as he appeared in the kitchen. Wilson thought they looked guilty. They had definitely been saying something they didn't want him to hear.

As the boys walked to school, Wilson tried to review the 12s in his head. But he still got stuck on them. He couldn't remember 12×8. Or 12×9. Or 12×11. And the more he thought about his parents' whispered conversation that morning, the more 12s facts he forgot.

It would be a miracle if he passed the 12s today.

It would be a miracle if he passed the 12s tomorrow.

It would be a miracle if he got his ice cream cone before he finished fifth grade.

When Mrs. Porter opened the door for the third graders, Wilson pushed ahead of everyone else into the classroom. Maybe if he could hold Squiggles for just a minute before class, he'd remember every single 12.

Squiggles wasn't in his cage. The door was open, and Squiggles was gone.

Had someone else already taken him? That was impossible. Wilson had been the first in line.

Was Squiggles off looking for more relief maps of Colorado to eat for breakfast?

"Mrs. Porter!" Wilson called out as she bustled to the front of the room. "Squiggles isn't here."

Mrs. Porter came over to the cage to look.

"The door was open," Wilson said. "Just like this."

"Oh, no," Mrs. Porter said, staring at the empty cage. "Maybe it wasn't closed all the way when we left school yesterday."

Wilson had a terrible thought. Had he been the last one to hold Squiggles? He had taken Squiggles out of his cage to celebrate passing the 9s, 10s, and 11s. Had he forgotten to latch Squiggles's door when he closed it?

"Let's not panic," Mrs. Porter said, looking ready to panic. "Class, take your seats." When everybody was sitting quietly, she asked, "Has anyone seen Squiggles?"

Nobody had.

"Laura, go check with the front office. Check with Cindy, too, if you can find her."

Cindy was the custodian. "See if anyone knows where Squiggles is."

Wilson stood for the flag salute, but he was too worried to do more than mouth the words. Hill Elementary was a very big school. Squiggles was a very small hamster. What if they never found Squiggles?

Wilson tried to remember yesterday afternoon. He had hugged Squiggles. He had put Squiggles back in his cage. He had shut the door. Had he latched it? Or not?

Laura returned, breathless. "No one's seen him," she reported.

"All right, class," Mrs. Porter said. "We'll need to make a special announcement on the intercom. If every student and every teacher at Hill Elementary is looking for Squiggles, he's sure to be found." But she didn't sound sure.

"Can we offer a reward?" Josh asked.

"Certainly. What should it be?"

"A million dollars," one boy suggested.

"I don't think our classroom treat fund has quite that much money in it," Mrs. Porter said.

"How about a leftover ice cream cone?" Becca suggested. "In case some people don't finish their 12s by tomorrow."

Wilson stared at his desk, hoping the rest of the class wasn't looking his way.

"Everyone *is* going to pass the 12s by tomorrow," Mrs. Porter said. "But that's a good idea. We do have some extra cones."

So Wilson's cone wasn't completely alone in the freezer. Was there someone else who hadn't passed his 12s? Somehow this thought wasn't much comfort now.

Then he had an idea, too. "I could draw a picture of Squiggles to put on the front bulletin board." Actually, his desk was already filled with doodled pictures of Squiggles. He opened his desk and grabbed the picture on top. "I have one right here."

"Excellent, Wilson!" Mrs. Porter said. "What a terrific picture. It looks exactly like him."

Wilson just hoped his picture would help.

Mrs. Porter sent Laura back to the office with their announcement and Wilson's artwork. A few minutes later, the principal's voice came over the intercom: "May I have your attention, please. Squiggles the hamster, class pet in Mrs. Porter's class, is missing. He is brown with a white face. A picture of him is posted on the front bulletin board outside the office. An ice cream cone reward is offered to anyone who can find him. Thank you all for your cooperation in looking for Squiggles."

For the rest of the day, whatever else Wilson did, he kept an eye and ear out for Squiggles.

He thought he heard a rustling in a corner of the art room. But it wasn't Squiggles.

He thought he saw something brown next to the piano in the music room. But it wasn't Squiggles.

He thought he felt something brush against his ankles in the cafeteria. But it wasn't Squiggles.

Wilson could hardly bear to look at Squiggles's empty cage. When he walked by the front office on the way to P.E., he had to look the other way so he wouldn't see Squiggles's picture. In the picture, Squiggles looked particularly lost and lonely.

After lunch, Wilson failed his 12s. Naturally.

9

Wilson studied his 12s that evening till he couldn't study them anymore. His father timed him. His mother timed him. Kipper timed him. Peck-Peck and Snappy timed him.

That night he dreamed he was doing times tables with Squiggles curled up on his lap. He almost had them all: he had done the 9s, the 10s, the 11s. But then suddenly Squiggles wasn't there, and Mrs.

Porter was looming over him, telling Wilson he couldn't go look for Squiggles until he could tell her the answer to 12×7.

"96," Wilson said to himself when he finally woke up. "No, 84. Or 72?"

"I'm sure you'll pass them," his mother said, pouring syrup on his toaster waffle. She sounded as unsure as Mrs. Porter had sounded yesterday about finding Squiggles.

"I know a secret," Kipper said. "I know a secret reason why you're going to pass them." Kipper definitely looked pleased with himself.

"What is it?" Wilson asked, not that he put much hope in any secret reason of Kipper's.

"I'm not telling," Kipper said. "If I told, it wouldn't be a secret."

"Wilson is going to pass them because

Wilson knows them," their father said. "Just relax, don't stress, and you'll do fine."

Relax? Don't stress? It had obviously been a long time since his father had taken a times-table test. At least his father's advice made Wilson remember to tuck some sharp new pencils in the outer pocket of his backpack. He had already eaten all the erasers off the last batch, stressing over the 3s, 4s, 5s, 6s, 7s, 8s, 9s, 10s, and 11s.

His backpack felt extra lumpy today, even though Wilson had no homework projects due. One of these days, he needed to clean out all the stray mittens and crumpled candy wrappers he had stuffed in there.

When the boys reached school, Wilson saw Mrs. Porter outside on playground duty, talking to Laura.

Wilson ran over to them. "Did anyone find Squiggles yet?" he asked.

"No," Mrs. Porter said. "I hope we find him today. I'd hate for him to be lost all weekend."

Wilson would hate that, too.

"Maybe he's in the cafeteria," Laura suggested. "Hamsters go where there's food."

"But there's no food there at night," Wilson said. "And nothing to do. I think he'd go to the art room. Remember how he liked our relief maps?"

"The library!" Wilson and Laura said together. The relief maps were all finished and painted and on display in the library. Maybe Squiggles was eating one of them right now. Wilson didn't care if Squiggles ate his map, ate his Rocky Mountains right down to the Great Plains, as long as they found him.

They turned to Mrs. Porter. "Can we go inside early?" Laura asked.

"We just thought of someplace to check for Squiggles," Wilson added.

"All right," Mrs. Porter said.

They raced to the library. But it was quiet and empty. There was no sign of Squiggles anywhere.

"I was so sure we'd find him here." Laura's voice sounded shaky with disappointment.

"Me too," Wilson said. "But we'll find him somewhere. We have to find him somewhere."

Because it was the last day to take times-table tests, Mrs. Porter let Wilson do one right after the flag salute. Jake Moran was taking one, too. So Wilson *wasn't* the only kid in the class who hadn't passed his 12s.

Still worried about Squiggles, Wilson had trouble concentrating. He knew he had failed even before he handed his paper to Mrs. Porter.

Jake passed his. So now Wilson *was* the only kid in the class who hadn't passed his 12s.

"Keep on studying this morning, after you finish your other work," Mrs. Porter told Wilson. "I'll give you another test this afternoon, and then, if you still need to do *another* one, I'll let you stay after school to do it."

Wilson mouthed the 12s under his breath all morning long. He was reading *Charlotte's Web* for silent reading. Fern sat in the barn talking to Wilbur the pig. 12 × 7 = 84. Templeton the rat ate the slops from Wilbur's trough. 12 × 8 = 96. Charlotte the spider sat spinning her web. 12 × 9 = 108.

At lunch, Wilson looked all around the cafeteria again for Squiggles, in case Laura was right. But the cafeteria was too noisy a place for a frightened little hamster.

After lunch, Wilson got ready to take the 12s test again.

He tried to relax. He tried not to stress. He hoped Kipper's secret would help him, whatever it was.

But he failed. He got the hard 12s right, all of them. But this time he missed two of the easy ones, 12×4 and 12×5.

"You're so close," Mrs. Porter told him. She looked as if she wanted Wilson to pass almost as much as he did. "Can you stay after school to try one more time?"

"Sure," Wilson said. He had to pass his test then, he just had to.

When the final bell rang, Josh gave Wilson a thumbs-up sign as he ran off with the others. Laura slipped him a piece of paper. On it, in her perfectly neat cursive, she had written, "Good luck!"

The classroom was oddly quiet now. No children's voices. No whirring of a Ferris wheel turned by scurrying little hamster feet.

"Ready?" Mrs. Porter asked.

Wilson picked up his pencil.

"Go!"

Wilson forced himself to concentrate as he had never concentrated before in his life. He wasn't a boy any longer. He was a multiplication machine, programmed to do times tables perfectly, effortlessly, with every single 12s fact right every single time.

Mrs. Porter snatched the test away as soon as Wilson had finished and scanned it with her eyes.

"You did it!" she crowed.

Wilson was about to give her a hug when the intercom clicked on. "Wilson Williams. Wilson Williams. Please come to the kindergarten room. Your brother is waiting for you."

Oh, no! In his last-ditch effort to pass the 12s, Wilson had forgotten all about Kipper. Kipper had been waiting the whole time at the kindergarten door. He was probably crying.

Wilson jumped up to go.

"Don't forget your backpack!" Mrs. Porter called after him. "And after you get your brother, go get your ice cream cone!"

Wilson didn't care about his ice cream cone now. He grabbed his backpack and unzipped it to jam his Friday folder inside.

Then he saw what had made his pack so lumpy that morning.

It was Peck-Peck.

Kipper's secret.

Wilson zipped his pack shut and ran off to get Kipper.

When Wilson reached the kindergarten room, Kipper wasn't crying, though he looked very little and left-behind.

"I'm sorry, Kipper," Wilson said. "I stayed to take the 12s one last time. And I passed them!"

"Good for you!" Mrs. Macky said. She had been Wilson's kindergarten teacher, too. "We figured you had to be somewhere in the building."

"Did you look in your backpack?" Kipper asked. "Did you find the secret?"

"I found Peck-Peck," Wilson said. "I passed just because of him!"

Well, not *just* because of Peck-Peck. Three weeks of constant study had helped. Having his whole family time him on practice tests had helped. So had Mrs. Porter's encouragement, and Josh's jokes, and Laura's 9s trick.

And being able to hold Squiggles right before a test. If only someone would find Squiggles before the long, lonely weekend.

"We can go get my ice cream cone," Wilson told Kipper. "You can have half of it."

He thought of how much Kipper—and Snappy and Peck-Peck—had rooted for him over the past three weeks. How proud Kipper had been of hiding Peck-Peck in

Wilson's backpack. Kipper couldn't help being good at math any more than he could help sometimes being pesky and annoying. Both were just Kipper being Kipper.

"You can have *all* of it," Wilson said.

"I have an idea," Mrs. Macky said. "Why doesn't Kipper have one of our kindergarten snacks instead? I think Wilson has earned that cone."

She led the way to the kindergarten snack closet. The door of the closet stood wide open. Mrs. Macky's room was always messy. It had been messy when Wilson was in kindergarten, and it was still messy now. The stuff on the closet shelves looked ready to tumble down. A bunch of fruit-and-grain bars had their wrappers partly torn off. Shredded bits of wrapper lay nearby.

Wilson looked at them again. Mrs. Macky was messy, but not *that* messy. She wouldn't just tear the wrappers off her fruit-and-grain bars and leave the torn-off pieces lying there.

He felt his pulse quicken.

Wilson looked once more at the mess on the closet shelf. One of the wrappers moved ever so slightly.

Wilson reached up and pushed the wrapper aside. There was Squiggles, looking not the slightest bit ashamed for gorging himself on stolen kindergarten snacks.

Wilson picked him up and hugged him. Squiggles didn't struggle or try to get away. Maybe he was relieved at being found, however much fun he had had in the snack closet.

"I can't believe it!" Mrs. Macky said. "I can't wait to tell our class on Monday."

Then she looked at her watch. "Listen, boys, it's getting late. Hurry back to third grade with Squiggles. And then I believe you have your reward cone to get, too, for finding him."

Two ice cream cones! Wilson had lost all hope of ever getting an ice cream cone. He never would have guessed he'd get two in one day.

Cradling Squiggles in his cupped hands, Wilson headed back to Mrs. Porter's room, with Kipper skipping along beside him. On the way, he stopped by the front office. Mrs. Bullert, the school secretary, gave him a red marker. Kipper held Squiggles while Wilson wrote on Squiggles's picture: FOUND!

"There you are!" Mrs. Porter said when they finally reached the third-grade room. "I was just on the phone with your mother."

Wilson felt a sudden pang of guilt. His mom must have been worried.

"And I was telling her— Oh, Wilson, did you find Squiggles?"

Wilson held Squiggles out for her inspection. He knew he was beaming.

Mrs. Porter collected Squiggles and gently returned him to his cage. "Look," she said, "the latch is loose. No wonder Squiggles kept escaping." She tied the door shut with a piece of string.

"Squiggles needs to go home with somebody this weekend," Mrs. Porter said then. "Would you boys like to take him again? If not, I can take him home with me."

"Yes!" Wilson shouted. "Kipper and I want Squiggles." He wished he could have a hamster at his house every single week-end of the year.

"Oh, by the way," Mrs. Porter went on, "your mother told me that she and your father talked yesterday about getting you boys a hamster of your own."

Wilson could hardly believe what he was hearing. Beside him, he could feel Kipper draw in his breath.

"She was wondering if I knew of any hamsters that needed a good home. And it just so happens that I do. Did you know Squiggles has a sister, Snuggles? They were born in the same litter. I've been caring for Snuggles at my house, but I'd be thrilled if you boys would take her."

Wilson couldn't answer over the lump in his throat, but Kipper answered for him. "Yay!"

"Don't forget your ice cream cones, now!" Mrs. Porter told them.

Wilson wouldn't forget; Kipper wouldn't let him. But he almost didn't care about his ice cream cone anymore.

Two brothers times one hamster of their own equaled happiness.

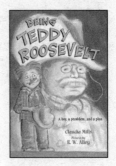